The MOOsic Makers
An original concept by author Heather Pindar
© Heather Pindar

Illustrated by Barbara Bakos

MAVERICK ARTS PUBLISHING LTD
Studio 3A, City Business Centre, 6 Brighton Road, Horsham,
West Sussex, RH13 5BB, +44 (0)1403 256941
© Maverick Arts Publishing Limited
Published July 2019

A CIP catalogue record for this book is available at the British Library.

Maverick
publishing

www.maverickbooks.co.uk

ISBN 978-1-84886-427-6

The MOOsic Makers

WRITTEN BY
HEATHER PINDAR

ILLUSTRATED BY
BARBARA BAKOS

Out on the wild, winsome hills, Joni sat
on her farmhouse porch, just listening.

Her cows were making music.

Celery's voice was round and mellow like an old apple barrel.

Nutmeg could make the mandolin tinkle and dance like a fresh

mountain stream.

"I love that old MOO-grass music," sighed Joni.

"Why can't we have mandolins and singing lessons?" grumbled Billy.

"Celery this, Nutmeg that," said Esme. "We're sick of hearing it!"

"Look at those clouds," said Joni.

"There's a storm coming."

The storm tore across the hills.

The rain battered Joni's rickety barn. The wind whirled the roof into the sky and carried it over the winsome hills and far, far away.

"I've no money for a new roof," sighed Joni.

"We'll help," said Celery.

"Us too!" said Billy and Esme.

But Nutmeg and Celery were already grabbing their checked shirts and straw hats and rushing off, to start...

...busking.

"What about us?" said Billy and Esme.

"You can hold my hat," said Celery.

Celery and Nutmeg busked and busked.

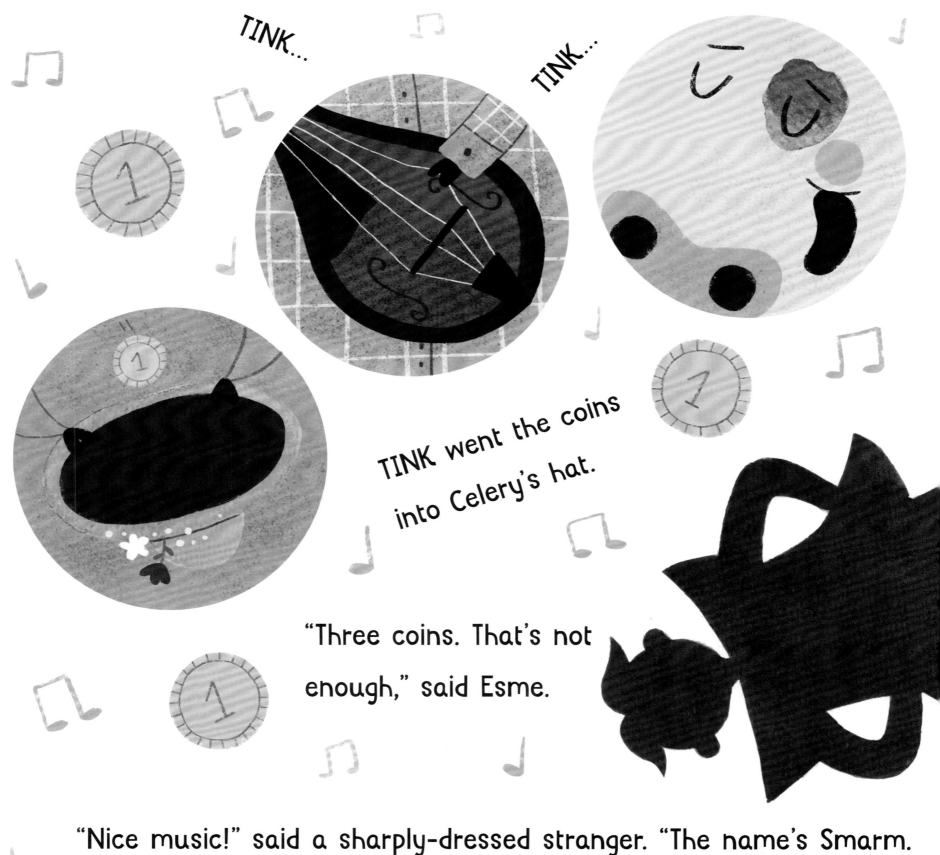

TINK...

TINK...

TINK went the coins into Celery's hat.

"Three coins. That's not enough," said Esme.

"Nice music!" said a sharply-dressed stranger. "The name's Smarm. Georgie Smarm. I can make you rich and famous, but..."

"...Forget MOO-grass music, DisCOW music is the thing. Checked shirts and straw hats are for *boys*. Think glittery sandals and pink dresses. *Trust* me."

"So DisCOW music will make us famous?" said Celery.
"And pay for a new roof," said Nutmeg. "Esme and Billy,
go back to the farm. You can leave everything to us!"

Nutmeg and Celery played every outhouse, schoolhouse, and henhouse in the county.

Soon everyone was talking about DisCOW Music.

Celery and Nutmeg played the megadromes.

They arrived by liMOOsine.

Makers! MOOOOOO!" chanted the crowd.

After every show Celery asked, "Will you pay us now?"

"Soon," Smarm always said...

...until after the twenty-seventh show Celery declared,
"Mr Smarm, we miss MOO-grass music, you STILL
haven't paid us and we can't stand pink. We quit!"

"MOOtiny?" sneered Smarm. "You wouldn't dare!"

"Watch us," said Celery.

"Let's get MOOOOOving!" said Nutmeg.

They trotted to the high road...

...stuck out their hooves and hitch-hiked home.

What a welcome they had!

"Sorry, everyone," said Nutmeg. "We only have three coins for the barn roof."

"But we'll raise more money," said Celery, "and this time...

...we're doing it OUR way."

"What we need," said Joni, "is a MOOsic Festival!"

"No," said Billy firmly, "we need a MOO-BAA-HEHAW-sic Festival!"

News of the festival spread fast.

Moo-Baa-Hehaw-sic Festival

The crowd went wild for...

...'Billy and The Funky Donkeys!'

'Esme and The Jersey Bleats',

and, of course, the 'MOOsic Makers'.

Moo-Baa-Hehaw-sic
Festival.

TINK!

TINK!

TINK!

TINK!

Went hundreds of coins into Joni's hat.

Enough for a barn roof...

...and mandolins and singing lessons for everyone.

"Smashing," said Joni, "har-MOO-ny at last."

THE END